A SHORT STORY BY
DANIEL ORTIZ

Charleston, SC
www.PalmettoPublishing.com

The Inbox

Copyright © 2020 by Daniel Ortiz

All rights reserved.

No portion of this book may be reproduced, stored in a retrieval system, or transmitted in any form by any means—electronic, mechanical, photocopy, recording, or other—except for brief quotations in printed reviews, without prior permission of the author.

First Edition

Paperback ISBN: 978-1-64990-450-8

ONE

THE INTENSE MID-AUGUST morning sun pierced through the living room casement windows, awakening Devon from a deep, drunken slumber. *Where the hell am I?* He quickly lifted his head from the sofa cushions; the effort made him dizzy. The brightness of the room made his eyes squint as he sat up on the couch. He leaned forward and placed both elbows on his knees. "Ugh, my head is pounding!"

He could hear soft music playing in the next room, what sounded like a pop rock song from the '90s.

Where is everyone?

He couldn't remember much of anything from the night before. In fact, the last thing he remembered was a few dozen rowdy fellows shouting, "Chug! Chug! Chug!"

Devon Owens had just celebrated his twenty-third birthday. He let out a small grunt as he reached up to caress his throbbing temples, feeling something strapped onto his head.

He quickly snatched it off to see that it was just a party hat. He chuckled when he realized he was at Elliot's house, his best friend. Elliot Vargas and Devon were more like brothers than friends.

He glanced around the room to see board game pieces scattered across the living room floor. Empty beer cans littered any flat surface available, and the air reeked of booze. *Uh-oh, I think I'm going to throw up.* Devon gripped his stomach.

"Well, look who's finally resurrected from the dead," Elliot said smoothly as he strolled into the room.

He wore a white muscle T-shirt tucked neatly into his skinny jeans; his right arm displayed in colorful tattoos. Elliot was much taller than Devon and very muscular too. He had no problem getting any girl he wanted, a definite ladies' man.

Holding a cold beer, Elliot chuckled as he sat down on the couch beside the hungover Devon.

"What happened last night?" Devon asked.

"Well, do you really want to know?" Elliot teased, scratching the hair on his chin.

"Uh, yeah, one moment we're playing a video game, the next minute, I'm surrounded by all these loud people."

Elliot took a sip of his beer. "First of all, you can rephrase 'all these people' because they were all your friends. All I can say is that you had the most fun I've seen you have in a while. Check your phone—you'll see I sent you some photos." He pointed at Devon's phone and took another sip. Devon grabbed the phone and began to look through the photos.

"Not bad for a surprise birthday party, huh?"

Devon laughed as he swiped through the photos.

"Ugh, this hangover is killing me. I can't remember a single thing after that last shot. I . . . wait a minute." Devon paused before remembering. "It was you!" He pointed his finger at a smiling Elliot. "It was you! You were the one who gave me that awful shot, weren't you?"

"Relax, it was all in good fun. What better way to celebrate than here at my place, waking up at 1 p.m. the next day!" Elliot smirked.

Devon instantly looked back down at his phone to check the time. "Holy mother of— Why didn't you wake me up sooner?" He sprang to his feet.

"I don't know—you looked so peaceful lying there in your sleep, kind of like a princess in her crown." Elliot laughed. "Oh, and you might want to check in with your folks. I think your mom was trying to reach you; your phone was buzzing all morning."

"Well, lucky you and I live a couple of blocks away from each other. I'll head home now—she'll know I'm alright when she sees me." Devon sat up to leave. "It's been real, E. Thanks again for the surprise party!"

Devon knew his parents wouldn't worry too much over his whereabouts. The Owenses were a tight-knit family and never hovered over him. Besides, summer break was nearly over, and they wanted him to enjoy his time while he was home. Devon would soon head back to his college dorm, just a few miles away from his folks and his girlfriend, Samara.

Devon and Samara had been dating since the seventh grade. They were a smitten pair. They'd always figure out a way to see each other during weekends when Devon was back on campus. Samara was on her way over, so once he arrived home, Devon went inside to wait for her.

As she strolled up to the Owenses' house, Samara saw Mr. Owens standing outside.

"Good day, Mr. Owens," she greeted.

Mr. Owens adjusted his glasses for a better look. "Well, look who we have here. If it isn't our favorite friend. How are you, Samara?"

Samara smiled. "I'm doing very well, thank you. I see you have quite a lot on your plate right now, or should I say porch?" she said politely.

"You know I've got to get these dried leaves off the porch before Li Na gets on my case again," Mr. Owens chuckled.

"Well, Mr. Owens, if you need any help with yard work, be sure to let me know. My little brother Timothy wouldn't mind raking up some leaves for you," she offered.

"Why, thank you, Samara! That is very kind of you. I'll definitely hold you to that offer." He held the door open for her to enter the house. "Now, don't you get any of this mess inside. I'll never hear the end of it from Li Na."

"I won't, I promise." Samara laughed.

Samara made her way into the living room, where she caught a whiff in the air of something delicious cooking.

"Is that Samara's voice I hear?" Mrs. Li Na Owens shouted from the kitchen.

"Yes, Mrs. Owens, it's me." Samara followed her nose into the kitchen.

"Oh, honey, how are you?" Mrs. Owens stretched out her arms to Samara, and they shared a tight hug. "I knew I heard your voice. You're just in time for lunch. Please help yourself to a bowl. I'm making broccoli cheddar soup."

"That sounds lovely, Mrs. Owens. But before I do, may I ask, is Devon home? I've been calling him all morning, but I haven't heard a word from him."

"Oh yes, honey," Mrs. Owens replied. "He just walked in a few minutes ago. Would you please get his attention for me and let him know lunch is ready? You know he only listens to you," Mrs. Owens winked.

"Of course, he does," Samara said sarcastically.

Samara walked down the hallway to Devon's bedroom door. She knocked gently and said hello. Getting no reply, she pushed the door open to find Devon in his gaming headset and underwear, playing a video game. Surprised, Devon removed his headset and sat up.

"Baby, I had no idea you'd drop by this early. Didn't you have an interview today?" He rushed over and kissed her softly.

"Were you ever going to return my calls?" Samara gave Devon a stern look.

"Ugh! Babe, you have no idea what happened to me," Devon replied. He sat on the edge of his bed and pulled on some pants and a T-shirt. "Last night, Elliot threw me a wild surprise birthday party. I got so wasted and wound up passing out on his couch. My phone died on my way home. I was going to call you, I swear. Forgive me?" He looked into Samara's eyes, pouting his lips.

Samara cracked a smile. "You are so annoying, Devon. How do you make it so easy for me not to be mad at you?" She sat beside him and placed a kiss on his cheek. "Oh, and by the way . . ." Samara paused as her eyes filled with excitement, "I got the job. You're now looking at the new flight attendant for Dream Sky Airlines!"

Devon clutched Samara. "YES! I knew you'd get it." Kissing her over and over, he heard his mom shout from the hallway: "Lunch is ready!"

"I'll be there in a minute, Mom," he yelled. "So, do you know what this means?" Devon raised an eyebrow.

"Hmm, I don't know. . . That I'm joining you guys for lunch today?" Samara said sarcastically.

"No, we have to celebrate tonight! Dinner and wine on me?"

"I think I like the sound of that, Dev."

They shared another kiss and playfully waltzed their way out of the room and into the kitchen.

After lunch, Samara headed home to prepare for her dinner date with Devon. Once she left, Devon lounged upstairs in his room. He lay on his bed and stared at the ceiling for hours, one hand behind his head and the other jammed in his pocket. Time seemed to go by quickly.

Oh damn, I should be getting ready. He leaped out of bed and began to scavenge his closet for an outfit for the night.

Just then, his laptop let out an unusually loud notification. *Could it be?* He swiftly moved to his desk and sat down. Devon couldn't ignore any messages with a possible lead; he was searching for an apartment. Dorm life was becoming a bit overwhelming, and it was about time for a change. He also couldn't wait to ask Samara to move in with him.

He opened his inbox and discovered a message from an unfamiliar sender, Belladonna. What a strange name. Devon stared at the computer screen for a moment, then quickly began to read.

Dear Devon,
I want to take this opportunity to introduce myself. My name is Belladonna. But you can call me Bella for short. I'm a realtor agent. I'd like to know if you would like to look at a beautiful apartment I have, waiting just for you! Keep in touch.

Devon tried remembering, but he had no recollection of who Belladonna was or if he had requested assistance from a realtor agent for his search. He also couldn't decline the offer; after all, he'd be that much closer to having his own place, finally. This meant he wouldn't have to go back to his tiny, shared dorm room. He took a deep breath as he made his decision.

Dear Bella,
This sounds great! I can't wait to get more information about this offer. I promise to keep in touch—you have my word.

That night, Devon took Samara to a fabulous Italian restaurant. It was romantic and dimly lit, the perfect place for a celebratory dinner.

"Do you like it here?" Devon asked, giving a wry grin.

"I don't like it—I love it." Samara gazed into Devon's eyes. She hesitated for a moment. "Is this in your budget?"

Devon laughed. "Are you trying to be funny?"

Samara shook her head, feeling giddy. "You are something else. You've really outdone yourself tonight."

They browsed the complicated menu and placed their orders.

"It's a special night. You're starting a new job, and I'm look—" Devon paused, realizing he almost mentioned the news about potentially finding a place. "I-I-I'm looking at the most wonderful flight attendant in the world," he stammered. "We've got so much to look forward to now. Cheers to that!" Devon raised his wine glass to Samara's. He planned to share the news with Samara at some point, but tonight didn't seem like the right time.

"So, am I allowed to order dessert too?" Samara asked.

Devon reached out and brought one of Samara's hands to his lips, gazing intensely into her brown eyes. "Yes, anything you'd like. Tonight is my treat."

In that moment of rooted satisfaction, Devon's phone chimed.

"Hey, I thought we said no phones on tonight," Samara scolded. Devon chuckled as he grabbed his phone and attempted to put it away before Samara stopped him.

"I'm just kidding, babe. Aren't you going to see who that was?" Samara gave Devon a quizzical stare.

"Not now. Tonight, is about you and me." Placing his phone on vibrate, he tucked it into his pocket.

"Would you like to take a look at our dessert menu for tonight?" the waiter asked as he collected their empty dinner plates. "We have our infamous 'sex in a pan' special, which is a favorite."

"Ooh, sounds delicious." Samara raised her eyebrows and grinned. "Yes!" She fixed her eyes on Devon. "We'll have one of those, but to go, please."

The smile tugging at Devon's lips broke into a grin. "What am I going to do with you, Ms. Thing?"

Samara broke out into laughter. "Thing? Excuse me, sir?" She rolled her eyes. "I think the proper way to address me is by calling me Your Royal Highness," she said, grabbing her glass of wine and swirling her finger around the rim.

Suddenly, Devon felt his phone vibrate through his pocket. He leaned back in his chair and reached for it.

"Did I say something wrong?" Samara asked, noticing a confounded expression on his face.

"No. I mean, yeah. Everything's fine, babe. I just received an email, probably spam." He took a quick peek at his phone and saw a new email notification. He quickly swiped over to his inbox and saw it was a message from Bella. *It must be important.* Devon wasn't ready to mention the news to Samara yet.

"Devon, did you hear me?" Samara asked and paused for a response. She continued when he didn't give one: "I asked if you are ready to go now. The dessert is packed." She waved a to-go box in the air.

"Oh yes, babe, let me just . . ." He paused and removed cash from his wallet. "There, now we can go." They stood from the table and made their way out of the restaurant.

Upon exiting, Devon felt a cold chill run down his spine, followed by an inaudible whisper from behind. Startled, he turned around to see where the sound had come from, but there was no one there.

"Babe, come on," Samara said, fiddling impatiently by the exit.

"Sorry, I'll be right there," Devon said in a quiet voice; his thoughts were everywhere but there.

TWO

THE NEXT MORNING, Devon awoke to the sound of his cell phone vibrating on his nightstand. He quietly reached for it, hoping not to wake Samara, who had spent the night. The phone had stopped vibrating by the time he picked it up. Looking at the screen, he had an anonymous missed call. *No caller ID? At this time?* In an instant, Devon's phone began to vibrate again in his hand.

Quickly sneaking outside his room, he answered the call, "This is Devon." He could hear heavy breathing on the other line but no reply. "Hello?" His voice grew louder. Confused, he pressed the phone hard against his ear. When he heard a low chilling growl, it startled him.

"Hey! Who is this?" he demanded.

Before he could get a response, Mrs. Owens called from down the hallway, "Hello!"

The phone immediately went dead. In a panic, Devon grabbed his chest, almost dropping his phone. "Whoa, Mom! You scared the living bejesus out of me!"

"Caught ya, didn't I," she laughed. "Are you hungry? I'm just about to start making breakfast. Did Samara spend the night?"

"Which question should I answer first?" Devon asked in a sarcastic tone.

"Oh my, aren't we quite the grumpy grouch this morning." Mrs. Owens raised her eyebrows. "Well, if you are hungry, breakfast will be ready in an hour. I'm making Samara's favorite—pumpkin pancakes."

Devon nodded his head and walked back to his room. He gently crawled into bed.

"So, who called?" Samara asked in a soft voice.

"Oh, you're awake?" Devon turned his body over and cuddled Samara close.

"Well, kind of," Samara replied with her face buried in Devon's chest. "The cell phone buzzing woke me. Who on earth wants to talk on the phone this early?"

"To be honest, I'm not quite sure. Wrong number, I guess," Devon replied with a chuckle.

"Strange. Do you have a secret admirer?" Samara lifted her face for an answer.

"No, not at all, babe."

"You sure it's not that girl from your computer class. What was her name again? Desiree?"

Devon unwrapped his arms from Samara and stared at the ceiling. "Are you talking about Delilah?"

"Yes! That girl. I never liked her."

Devon smiled and reached over to lay a kiss on Samara's cheek. "You have nothing to worry about, babe. By the way, Mom's making your favorite—pumpkin pancakes."

Samara gave Devon a tender smile. "Okay, you got me there. Let's go." They went downstairs and started their day.

Later that afternoon, Devon checked in with Elliot at his place.

"What's up, Dev?" They gave each other a fist bump. "Are you ready to shoot some hoops today?" Elliot grabbed two bottles of water from the refrigerator; he tossed one to Devon.

"Sure, only if you're looking to get your ass whipped." Devon leaped from his chair and ran out the back door into the yard; Elliot chased right behind him.

After a quick game of one-on-one, the boys sat on the ground of the basketball court, sweating and out of breath.

"So . . . are you ready to head back to campus?" Elliot asked.

"I guess," Devon responded unsurely, removing the cap from his water bottle.

"What is it?" Elliot asked with genuine concern.

"I mean, I am ready. But not too thrilled."

"Why the hesitation?"

"Well, I'm thinking of asking Samara to—"

"Well, it's about damn time!" Elliot interrupted. "Finally! You're going to marry Samara, right? Dude, the two of you are made for each other! You guys have been dating since you were, what, twelve years old? I just hope you know that I'll be the best man at the wedding." He shrieked with laughter.

Devon laughed, shaking his head. "You didn't let me finish. I'm actually planning to ask her to move in with me."

"Oh? Well, that's great too! So, have you found a place?"

"Yes. Well, I mean, not exactly." Devon's phone chimed. Loudly.

"Damn, that's awfully loud, bro," Elliot said while covering one ear. "Is it Samara?" He pointed at Devon's phone as he stood up and began to dribble the basketball.

"No," Devon answered. He saw it was a new inbox message. He began to read:

Dear Devon,
I'm hoping we can set up a time to talk over the phone today to go over some very important information.
Sincerely, Bella

"Well, who is it then?" Elliot asked, dribbling the ball.

"Oh, it's just Bella, a realtor I've been chatting with."

Devon turned a perplexed gaze at Elliot. "So, is everything cool? Why do you look so confused?"

"Oh, nothing, I . . ." Devon hesitated before continuing, "I just don't recall signing up to have an agent reach out to me. I'm not sure how it happened. I have no idea who I'm even talking to," he chuckled softly.

Elliot ran his fingers through his dark curly hair, resting the basketball on one hip. "Well, remember. You might have your own place before classes start. It's time to say goodbye to that tiny dorm, bro." He dribbled the basketball fast and made a shot. "Score!" he shouted. "So, are we on for game two, or are you quitting on me now?" Elliot leaped in the air and made another shot. Devon got up and shook off the uncertainty he was feeling as they began to play their second game.

By the time Devon decided to walk home from Elliot's, it was sunset. He suddenly remembered he hadn't replied to the email Bella sent him earlier that day. He pulled out his phone and began to type.

Bella, we can set up a time to talk over the phone. I am available to talk now if that is okay.

Instantaneously, he received another alarming chime. *Gosh, I really need to change that sound.*

Devon felt a cold chill run down his spine. He couldn't help but think about the last time he got the exact same chill. It was the same feeling he'd had at the restaurant—as if someone was watching him. Dead leaves swept across the concrete sidewalk toward him in a sudden gust of cold wind. He shivered, sensing something evil in the air; he looked around, finding nothing but an empty street. He checked his phone again—there was another inbox message from Bella.

Dear Devon,
It's so nice to hear from you. Please send your phone number, and I'll give you a call.

Devon replied immediately this time, giving his phone number, and continued his way home. Seconds later, his phone rang; the caller was private.

Should I answer an unknown call? Could this be Bella? He hesitantly answered.

"Um, Devon here."

"Hello there, Devon," a woman's voice greeted.

"Yes, who is this?"

After an awkward moment of silence, she replied, "It's Bella. I'm calling to run through a few questions with you, as I mentioned in my email. Is that okay?"

"Yeah, I mean, of course."

"Okay, perfect. So, we'll do this quickly. I must first ask, are you a smoker?"

"Uh, no, I do not smoke."

"Okay. We don't like smokers in our residence. We love a healthy lung." Bella's voice was youthful and cheery. "How much do you weigh, Devon?" Her tone grew sharp.

"Uh, I-I'm about 160." Devon stuttered.

"Mmm, that's delightful. And how tall are you, Devon?"

He swallowed hard at the question. Something suddenly felt off about the conversation. *Why would she ask me that?* He simply evaded the question.

"Anyway, I don't believe the neighbors will have any kind of trouble with me."

"Of course. That's good to know, Devon. Sorry for bombarding you with these questions, but you know, I've got to ask; it helps me get a good picture."

"Don't worry, I understand, I guess. Is there anything else you'd like to ask me?" Approaching his house, Devon took a seat on the front steps.

"Why, yes, just one more question, Devon. Are you single?"

"Well, I do have a girlfriend who will be moving in with me. I hope couples aren't a problem at the residence."

There was an uncomfortable silence for several seconds.

"NO!" Her voice sounded scratchy and deep.

Devon pulled the phone away from his ear. *Was that an animal? Or perhaps bad phone reception?*

"Hello? Are you there?" Devon hesitantly brought the phone back to his ear to hear Bella's sweet, upbeat voice again.

"I'm so sorry. I think I lost you for a second," she giggled. "There is definitely space for two. I'll set you up for a tour soon. Sound good?"

"Most definitely. I'm looking forward to it."

"It is my pleasure, Devon. Oh, but I must add one thing," she said in a stern voice.

"Yes?" Devon entered his house.

"To maintain the privacy of our tenants living in the building, it is important you arrive alone once we set up your tour date."

"Oh, okay." Devon's tone was understanding.

"Well then, this went better than I expected. We'll keep in touch. Goodbye, Devon." Bella hung up the phone.

Everything about this chilly Friday night was unusual. Devon found himself just staring into space, listening to the sound of the wind ruffling the leaves of the trees outside his window. His phone chimed again—it was Bella.

I do apologize for emailing you so late. I know we spoke earlier, but I was hoping you'd be available to meet with me this Sunday.
PS I thought I should mention, my tours do come with a very special snack.

Snack? Sweet! Devon began typing a reply.

Snacks are my favorite—you can surely count me in. And Sunday is excellent. Please send me the exact location and time for us to meet.

The next morning, Devon woke to the sound of his phone vibrating on his dresser. He had missed nine calls with no caller ID. He was barely awake. *Nine calls? It's way too early for this.* He buried his head back into his pillow as he heard birds chirping outside his window. An eerie silence echoed throughout the room. Suddenly, Devon heard a chilling voice whisper in his ear. The hairs on the back of his neck rose, and a loud thud hit his window. He immediately jumped out of bed in a panic. "WHAT WAS THAT!" he shouted.

He pulled the curtains aside but didn't see anything unfamiliar. He glanced around the room and noticed the bedroom door had been left ajar. He couldn't remember leaving it that way before he went to bed. Devon took another look out of his window and could see a thunderstorm coming. *Maybe it was just the rumbling thunder.*

A startling noise could be heard as the wooden floorboards creaked loudly from inside the closet.

"Is there someone in here?" he asked hesitantly. He turned around and slowly tiptoed to the closet. His heart was beating fast as he approached the closet door and prepared to open it forcibly on the count of three. *One . . . two . . .* He suddenly felt the presence of something standing behind him. He turned his head slowly over his shoulder and could see it sway from the corner of his eye. "Oh my GOD!" Devon yelled.

Mrs. Owens was standing in the doorway, dressed in a black bathrobe and fluffy white slippers.

"MOM, WHAT THE HELL! Can't you knock?" Devon squeezed his fists tightly, taking a deep breath.

"Oh my, Devon! You know, you've been so on edge these days," Mrs. Owens's voice cracked.

Devon cleared his throat and exhaled loudly, "I'm sorry, mom. You just frightened me, that's all."

"Well, would a cup of coffee help calm your nerves?" She grinned.

Devon walked over to his closet door and threw it open. There was nothing there. "Umm, yeah, I'll have some. I'll be right out, Mom."

She walked out of Devon's bedroom, reaching to shut the door behind her. Devon stopped her. "Leave the door open, would you!"

Mrs. Owens turned to Devon suspiciously. "Is something bothering you, Son?"

Devon sat on the side of his bed. "I'm sorry. Mom, do you ever get the feeling you're being watched?"

His mother stood in the doorway. "Of course, I do. By your father, *all* the time."

Devon gave a short smile. "No, Mom, have you ever felt like you were being watched by someone other than Dad?"

Mrs. Owens sat beside her son. "Do you want to tell me what's really going on?"

He hesitated. "Well, these past couple of days, I've been getting all kinds of unknown phone calls."

She interrupted, "Ooh could it be a secret admirer? Maybe it's that girl from your class. What's her name again? Damaris?"

"Mom, this is not about anyone from class."

"Oh, I'm sorry, I just don't like to see you like this," she said in a soft tone.

Devon let out a deep sigh. "I know, Mom. Neither do I. I don't know who could be behind this. When I answer, there's never any reply. Sometimes I can hear breathing on the other end. It's beginning to freak me out. I've never dealt with this before." Devon paused for a few seconds. "The calls started ever since I gave my number to this realtor agent online."

"Oh, honey," Mrs. Owens said. "You're looking for a place?" Her eyes widened.

Devon nodded his head. "Mom. It's about time; I'm twenty-three now."

Mrs. Owens chuckled. "Well, Son, perhaps it's just one of those websites you've signed up on?"

"But the websites I've signed up on are for applicants to choose their own agent, not the other way around, Mom. She chose me. I just don't know why." He looked around the room.

"Well, Devon, take this as a blessing that's showed up right at your front door. Maybe this is the place meant for you." She smiled and nodded at him. "You shouldn't worry, Son."

"You know, you're right, Mom. I'm in way over my head. Forget about everything I said. I'll be all right."

Mrs. Owens kissed his forehead. "Yes, you will. I'll see you in the kitchen?"

"Yes, Mom." Devon grabbed his cell phone and saw that it was 7:45 a.m. *I'm up way too early for a Saturday.* As soon as he put his phone down, he felt it vibrate. He lifted it to see an early-morning message from Bella.

Good morning, Devon.
I really can't wait to have you tomorrow.

Ugh, not this early. I'll respond later. He made his way to the kitchen, where his mom had coffee ready.

"I thought you went back to bed," she said, leaning over the kitchen counter, handing Devon his coffee.

"No, I think I'm up for the day," he said in a quiet voice.

Mrs. Owens nodded her head. "So, aside from the one realtor you mentioned, how is the rest of your search going, dear? I wish you had told me sooner that you were looking for a place. Your dad and I can make a few calls for you if you'd like."

"It's going pretty well, Mom. And honestly, no hard feelings, but I'd rather do this on my own."

Mrs. Owens smiled. "My boy is all grown up." She took a big swallow from her large coffee mug, a gift she received from Devon when he was in the fourth grade.

"I actually have an appointment to see a place tomorrow." Noticing the sad look on his mother's face, he changed the subject. "Anyway, what are you doing this weekend, Mom?"

He could see the excited change in her mood.

"Well, I'm glad you asked. Your dad and I are going to your Aunt Louisa's for a few days. Aunt Louisa and your Uncle Joseph just bought a marvelous place on a beautiful lot overlooking a lake." She paused. "On second thought, maybe you can drive up and join us, you know . . . right after you're done with your tour? There's plenty of room for you and Samara. What do you say?"

"No, I think I should stay," Devon replied. Mrs. Owens's face clouded over with sadness. "I've got a few things I need to work on here," Devon said, turning his head away.

"Well, I am very happy for you, Son. Go ahead and take care of what you need to do. The time is now." She walked over and hugged him tightly. "We should be leaving here by five o'clock today."

Later that afternoon, Devon's phone rang. It was Samara.

"Hello, my princess," he answered.

"Devon, are you kidding me!" Samara yelled.

Confused, he replied, "Am I in trouble or something?"

"Yes! Why would you post something like that online?" Samara exclaimed.

Baffled, Devon replied, "I have no idea what you're talking about."

"Look online! I can't believe this is how you feel about me!" she demanded as her voice cracked.

Devon stood up from his chair, checking through his laptop. He logged on to his social media to find that someone had posted to his account.

It read: *Samara, we are done. I'm sorry to call you out this way, but I've met someone new. Someone who isn't embarrassing to be with, you pathetic lowlife!*

THREE

A PENETRATING SHOCK froze Devon. He became flustered, trying to gather up the right words to say. "Samara, I did not write that! You got to believe me, okay! Listen, I've been getting all these weird calls. I've been talking to this girl named Bella."

Samara laughed. "Bella! Oh, so there *is* someone else. Is that what you're trying to tell me?" Her voice struggled with tears.

"Samara, no. Not in that way. I mean, it's a long story. I've been going back and forth talking to this agent. Ever since I gave her my number, weird shit has been going on. I need you to believe me and calm down for just a second."

Samara's voice quavered. "You want me to calm down? You know what, Devon, I am done. I cannot believe you would humiliate me like this after all we've been through!" She hung up abruptly before Devon could respond.

"Samara! No, please I . . ." Devon stared at his phone in disbelief. He tried to redial Samara's number, but the call went straight to voicemail. He left her a message.

"Samara, please call me back. This is crazy. I would never do something like that."

The room began to spin. Devon could feel a huge lump in his throat as his heart pounded faster. He propelled himself into his desk chair and spun around and around. He covered his eyes with his hands and dragged them down roughly to his chin. *Did I just lose my girlfriend?*

He grabbed his cell phone and decided to send a text instead. *Samara, I need you to call me back, please!* He took a deep breath.

Just as everything seemed to fall apart, he heard a holler from his dad: "We're about to get on the road, Son. Come on down."

Devon sprang from his chair and hurried downstairs to find his parents waiting at the doorway.

"There's some leftover spaghetti in the fridge from yesterday, still fresh. In case you get hungry later," Mrs. Owens said while placing a kiss on Devon's cheek.

Mr. Owens patted Devon on his shoulder. "Now, we'll call you once we get there. Don't burn the place down," he joked.

The Owenses walked out to their car. Devon paused in the doorway and watched his mom and dad drive off.

He went back inside the house and shut the door behind him. He tried to think of a way to convince Samara to believe him. *Who could have done this?*

He made his way up the stairs and had nearly reached the

top when a knock sounded at the door. He rushed back down and looked through the peephole. He couldn't see anyone.

He took a deep breath and opened the door, searching the front yard, but no one was there. He walked back into the house and slammed the door. He squeezed his eyes closed, taking a deep breath. *Relax, Devon.*

He heard his cell phone ringing from upstairs. He rushed up the stairs to his room, hoping it was Samara. Anxiously answering, he stuttered, "Ba-Babe-Baby, I'm so glad you called back . . . Hello?"

He heard heavy breathing, then a chilling voice spoke, "We are all alone now."

Frightened, he pulled the phone away from his ear to see it was the unknown caller.

"If you don't stop playing these games, I will find you and hurt you!" he shouted into the phone. There was a brief silence on the other end, quickly followed by a menacing laugh. Devon hung up the call and rushed to his bedroom door, slamming it shut.

He leaned his back against the door. *What was that?* He got up, sat in his chair, and called Elliot.

"Yo, what's up, Dev?" Elliot answered.

"Hey, man, not much. Are you home?" Devon swallowed the lump in his throat.

Elliot could hear the consternation in Devon's voice. "Is everything all right?"

"Yeah, I'm fine, bro." He hesitated for a moment, "No. I'm not fine. I think Samara just broke up with me. Can you come over now?"

"Alright, I'll be over in ten minutes," Elliot replied. Devon hung up.

How the hell do I explain something like this to someone? And how am I ever going to get Samara to believe it wasn't me who wrote that message online? He stared at his computer screen when he saw a new notification appear in his inbox. *Who the hell could that be now?* He opened the email to find that it was a message from Bella. *What could she possibly want?* He opened his inbox and read.

Hello Devon,
I'd like to confirm our meeting for tomorrow. I'm also including the address in this email . . . I can't wait.

"Is she kidding? Now isn't the time, Bella." Devon said aloud. Before he could reply, his bedroom door began to rattle. Staring at the doorsill, he saw what appeared to be a shadow underneath the door.

"Hello, who's there?" Devon's voice trembled. The rattling stopped, but there was no answer. *This is just nuts!* Devon got up and charged at the door with enough force to tear it off its hinges. Screws flew off the wall as he tried to grab the door before it banged to the ground.

"I said, Who's there!" Devon shouted from the empty doorway. He stepped into the hall and sped downstairs to the front door; it was closed. "Hello, Mom? Dad?" he yelled. Devon swiftly made his way into the kitchen but stumbled against a wooden stool. "Ow! DAMN IT!" he cried out, holding onto his foot.

He shook his head and started his way up the stairs when suddenly, a cold shiver ran down his spine. The front door creaked open. Beyond frightened, Devon missed a step and stumbled on the stairs.

There was no intruder. It was just Elliot.

"What the hell, Elliot!" Devon yelled.

Startled, Elliot dropped a six-pack case of beer. "Whoa! Dev! What the hell, you scared me!"

Devon burst into nervous laughter and skipped down the stairs to give Elliot a handshake. "What's up, E?"

"I don't know, man. You tell me. You look like you've seen a ghost or something. Is everything cool?"

Devon shut the front door and followed Elliot into the kitchen.

Elliot cracked open two cans of beer. "So, do you want to tell me what's going on with you and Samara and why you're all shaken up?" he asked as he handed a beer to Devon.

"There's just been a lot of weird things happening around me all day today." Devon popped the lid and took a sip of his beer as he wandered off into deep thought.

"So, do you want to talk about it or not? No pressure. We can drink it away, too," Elliot said.

"No, I'll share it with you. Just don't think I'm crazy." Devon's smile faded as he took another sip.

"Dev, just spit it out. What is going on?"

"All right, I'll tell you." Devon paused before continuing. "You ever get this weird feeling that something evil is out to get you?"

Elliot began to laugh so hard his eyes filled with tears. "I'm sorry. What'd you just say? Because I thought this was about

Samara." Elliot shook his head in disbelief, wiping tears from his eyes.

"I know it sounds bizarre. But I need you to hear me out without joking." He turned his back to Elliot, looking into his reflection in the kitchen window.

"I apologize. It's just . . . never mind. Please continue," Elliot said.

Devon faced his friend. "Do you remember the realtor I told you about the other day named Bella?"

"Yeah, the online stranger lady, right?"

"Yes, her. Anyway, we've been emailing about setting up a tour for this Sunday, and I know this may sound like I've gone mad, but something about her doesn't seem quite right."

"How so?"

"For starters, how did she find me?" Devon crossed his arms.

Elliot stared at him intensely. "Do you feel that Bella could just be stalking you?"

"I don't know. Maybe? Look, she only calls me from an unknown caller ID, and lately, that's all I've been getting: unknown calls from a no caller ID. I'm beginning to think Bella's behind the whole thing. Oh, and did I mention . . . my social media account got hacked today by someone posing to be me. I might've lost Samara because of it. I know it sounds crazy." He began to pace up and down the kitchen.

"Well, the only way to find out is if you meet with her," Elliot said. "Go and see for yourself whether she means real business or if she's just some crazy psycho serial killer you came across on the web who's out to gut you." Elliot laughed and grabbed another beer.

Devon gaped in fear. "Why would you say something like that?"

"Hey, listen, relax. You're all right. Don't be a wuss. I can go with you to this place on Sunday if you'd like."

"You can't come," Devon said in a low voice. "What do you mean? "Elliot asked curiously.

"I'm not sure. Bella said something about the privacy of the residents in the building or something like that. I don't know why, but you can't be there," Devon explained.

"Well, excuse me for trying to help out a friend," Elliot laughed as he leaned forward on the kitchen counter. "How about this then—if you send me the location, I'll drop you off on Sunday, and I'll stick around until the tour is over. Sound good?"

Devon nodded in agreement.

"This could all be in your head. You're probably stressed about the move, it's a big change to consider, you know? Also, maybe you did sign up for an agent, and you just can't remember 'cause your brain is fried from all of them video games you play," Elliot continued as he gulped down his second beer. He wiped his mouth with the back of his hand and let out a huge belch. "Whoa, excuse me!"

"I think you're right, E. I'm not going to sweat it anymore," Devon said.

"Okay, so we are on for Sunday?" Elliot asked as he zipped his jacket.

"You got it, E."

Elliot patted Devon on the back and headed home.

Devon stared at the empty doorway of his bedroom,

looking at the door lying on the floor in the hallway. *I'll fix that in the morning.*

He stepped into his room and checked his phone. He found a couple of unknown missed calls. *It's not a big deal; it's all in your head.* He exhaled and sat in his chair. He logged on to his laptop and confirmed his appointment with Bella for Sunday, which was the following day.

Hey Bella,
I am looking forward to tomorrow. How's 5:30 p.m.? See you then.
Dev

Instantaneously, Devon received a reply.

I can see you, Dev.

"I can see you?" Devon said aloud, and he snapped his head back, slowly turning in his chair to see if there was someone else in the room. He raked his fingers through his hair, taking a deep breath, and remembered the advice Elliot gave him. *Relax, you're just being paranoid. Maybe what she meant to say was I can't wait to see you.* He contemplated whether he should sleep in his parents' bedroom for the night. Something about sleeping in a room with an empty doorway didn't feel right, but he decided to stay in his own room.

Later that night, Devon tried to give Samara another call; she still didn't answer. He placed his phone upon his dresser and played video games to keep himself awake, in case Samara called.

After a long night of gaming with no calls or messages, he decided to get some rest. "All right, guys, I'm heading out now. I've got to get some sleep," Devon said to his online buddies. He removed his headset and shut down his gaming system. Still sitting in his chair, he glanced back toward his empty doorway. *Hmm. Creepy.* He decided to pay it no mind as he got into bed and quickly fell asleep.

FOUR

DEVON COULD SENSE an evil presence and instantly awoke from his sleep. He was afraid to move or make a sound. The room plunged into complete darkness when a tall, dark figure appeared from the shadows. Its bulging eyes glowed as it stood watching him from the empty doorway. Devon clenched his sheets tight. *GET OUT! GET OUT! GET OUT!* He thought he screamed aloud, but no sound came out. His eyes circled the room for help but came up empty. As he glanced in the mirror beside his bed, he began to frantically reach for his mouth. The mirror showed it had been sewn shut. He whimpered. *This isn't real!* He could hear his own breathing as he tried to shake out of the haunting sleep paralysis. *I need to wake up.* He depended on his inner voice to free him from his nightmare.

Turning his eyes to the doorway, he noticed the demon had disappeared. *Is it over?* Devon struggled to move. *Why can't I move?*

The demon manifested itself again. This time it stood at the edge of Devon's bed and grinned as it clambered slowly onto his body.

Devon could feel the weight of the demon pressed onto him as he lay in bed, paralyzed. *Why can't I breathe?* He panted heavily.

Finally, Devon gained movement in his feet. He could now tilt his head up toward the demon. He stared as it sat on his chest; hell stared deep into his soul. The demon then leaned forward and snarled down into Devon's face. He could feel its warm breath as it sniffed at his skin. The demon rapidly jerked its head back and let out a howling, diabolical screech. It was the same sound Devon had heard on the phone.

It quickly dropped its head and stared fixedly into Devon's eyes. Leaning into Devon's ear, it whispered, "We are all alone now." It lifted its head to look at him and let out a menacing laugh, stretching its hands to clutch his throat.

In an instant, Devon gained complete control over himself. He opened his mouth and screamed with all his might, "GET OUT!"

The demon instantly vanished in a cloud of thick, black smoke. Trembling, Devon managed to roll his body over, falling face down on his bedroom floor.

The room once again filled with sunshine, going back to normal as he rolled onto his back. *I'm alive.* He gasped for air.

What a horrible nightmare. He took another deep breath and lifted himself from the floor. His phone began to ring.

It was Samara. Devon answered immediately, still breathing heavily. "Babe, I thought you'd never call."

There was a moment of silence. "Hi, Devon. I've been thinking, and I want to apologize for how I reacted yesterday. I think I needed some time to think things through. Anyway, I am feeling much better today. Can we meet up and talk?"

"Yes. I would love that!" Devon exclaimed happily. "Samara, I don't want to lose you over something silly."

"I know, Dev. I want to believe you. I know you'd never do anything to hurt me."

"And you're absolutely right, Samara." Devon sat on the edge of his bed. "Can you swing by in a few? Let's say in about half an hour—or now if you want to?"

"Well, right now wouldn't work. I've got to go in for some background tests this afternoon for my new job," Samarra said.

"Oh. Right," Devon's voice lowered.

"But we could totally meet up afterward. It shouldn't take too long."

Devon suddenly remembered he'd be meeting with Bella later that same day. He hesitated for a few seconds.

"So, is that a yes?" Samara asked.

"Yes!" Devon replied. "Can you meet me at Café Rewind? You know, the place you like so much."

"Sure, sounds like a plan. Let's aim for five o'clock then," Samara said. Devon agreed, and they both hung up.

Feeling content, he nearly forgot about the horrific demon

encounter. *I've really got to stop playing those zombie games before bed.*

Devon sat at his desk to think of ways he could fit both things into his schedule. He came up with a proposition to meet Samara later that day because he had no intention of rescheduling his appointment with Bella. He picked up the phone and called Elliot; the call went straight to voicemail, so he sent his friend a text:

E! Thanks again for your advice yesterday. You were right; this stuff was all in my head. In other news, I thought you'd be happy to know that Samara gave me a call this morning and wants to talk. Please meet me at the café today, half past four.

Elliot replied: *Alright, I'll see you there.*

Later that day, Devon threw on a light jean jacket as he headed out to meet with Elliot. There was a cool breeze in the air. He passed by his old neighbor, Ms. James, who was getting a head start on her fall decorations.

"Good day, Ms. James," Devon called.

She turned around to see Devon waving hello. "How are you?" she asked. She peered over her large glasses and walked hesitantly toward Devon. She wore all types of unusual jewelry: crystals around her neck and varicolored beads around her wrists. She was old, harmless, and peculiar.

When Devon was young, the kids in the neighborhood would come up with horrifying stories that Ms. James was an evil witch who chopped up her husband and fed him to alley cats. Of course, those were just rumors, but some still believed them to be true.

Ms. James's house was surrounded by dry and dead branches. Ivy wrapped itself all the way up to the attic. It was an unusual sight in the neighborhood, especially compared to the other houses on the street. Stray cats would sunbathe in her front yard; some were sick with bald patches on their fur. They would creep their way through the decaying wooden fence into her garden. Poor Ms. James was too fragile to handle repairs.

"I'm doing well, Ms. James. How about yourself?" Devon asked, jamming his hands into his pockets.

Ms. James raised her head and stared deeply into Devon's eyes. "You've got something coming for you," she warned.

"What do you mean?" Devon asked, lowering his eyes.

She rummaged deep into her pockets and handed a strange ring to Devon. It was silver and set with a black oval stone. "Take this; it's an onyx ring, good for protection. I think you're going to need it." Before Devon had a chance to respond, she walked away.

Devon analyzed the ring. *Vintage, yeah, I like vintage.* "Thank you," he shouted, waving the ring in the air, hoping she heard it on her way. He walked away, squeezing the ring tightly in his hand.

Putting the ring in his pocket, Devon got into his car. The phone rang; it was Elliot.

"Hey, what's up?" Devon said.

"What do you mean what's up?" Elliot said. "I'm here, waiting on you. Where the hell are you? I thought we agreed to meet at four-thirty."

Devon could hear distinct chatter in the background. "I'm a few minutes away. I should be there in no time. I got caught up with Ms. James."

"What?" Elliot cackled. "I don't believe you; you're joking. The creepy old lady?"

"Yeah, I know, weird, huh. She gave me an onyx ring and said it's good for protection. I'm not even sure what to do with it."

"Protection? Did she mean *proposal*?" Elliot laughed.

"Very funny, E. I'll see you in a few." Devon smiled and hung up the phone.

Café Rewind had always been one of Samara's favorite spots. There were portraits on the walls and a large mirror that exaggerated the size of the cozy room. Anytime they'd visit, Samara always ordered her usual—a large apple cinnamon latte with extra whipped cream on top.

Devon walked through the door, and the shopkeeper's bell chimed. He saw Elliot seated, waiting with both arms crossed.

"Hey, sorry about that." Devon pulled out a chair.

"No, don't worry. I mean, I didn't know you and old lady James had some kind of fling going on. Is this why you and Samara aren't working out right now?" Elliot joked.

"No, it has nothing to do with Ms. James," Devon said. "Listen, Samara never really broke up with me, okay? She called me this morning and apologized."

Elliot gestured a silent round of applause.

Devon continued, "She wants to meet with me today. So, I invited her here to the café to talk." Devon glanced at his watch.

"Wait, so should I leave? Am I really third-wheeling right now?" Elliot asked, pointing a finger at himself.

"No, I don't want you to leave."

"But aren't you supposed to go see this apartment today?" Elliot asked with a puzzled look on his face.

Devon grabbed his cell phone from his pocket. "Yes! It's four forty-five now; the viewing is at five-thirty. I'll send you the location in a moment. I need you to stall Samara here—just for some time while I check out the apartment. If she asks, you can tell her I stepped out, and I'll be back with a surprise."

"Surprise? What are you going to get her?" Elliot asked.

"I don't know yet." Devon looked around the room and spotted a white rose standing in a table centerpiece. He grabbed the rose, handing it to Elliot.

Elliot side-eyed Devon. "Umm. All joking aside, are you feeling okay? Should I call you a doctor?"

"Yes, I am fine. Just give her this rose when she walks in. Tell her it's from me; it should buy me some time—she loves roses, especially white ones. I hope this goes well. Today, I'm going to ask her to move in with me, so don't ruin it."

"You have my word. I won't say anything." Elliot surrendered his hands in the air. "I'll just sit here and distract her. You got it." Elliot winked.

Devon nodded his head. "Yes, and when I'm back, you're free to go."

Devon stood up and patted his jean pockets. "Here you go." He pulled out a twenty and placed it on the table.

Elliot grabbed the money and gave it a whiff. "Ooh, and I'm getting paid, too? I could get used to this."

Devon snatched the bill from Elliot's hands. "Bro, this is so Samara can order whatever she wants. Better yet, I'll order what she likes and have it sent here to the table."

Elliot chuckled and shook his head. "Well, while you're at it, make whatever you're ordering for her a double."

Devon turned away and started toward the cashier when suddenly he got that feeling again—that someone was watching. A chill ran through his body. He stopped in the middle of the room and looked around. Everyone around him seemed to move in slow motion. A blurred view of someone passing by the café stood out. *Who is that?*

Devon's eyes widened as he looked through the large front window. The mysterious person was cloaked in a black hood. He couldn't make out an appearance since the hood covered the face entirely. Pausing at the window, the figure slowly turned and gave Devon a dark smile that sent chills through his body. The mysterious person then ran off.

Devon blinked hard several times. He saw that Elliot had been watching him the entire time.

"Hey! Did you see that?" Devon shouted across the small café.

"No," Elliot mouthed while shaking his head.

"Excuse me, sir?" Devon could hear someone calling to him. He realized it was the barista. She rolled her eyes, "I said, what can I get for you?"

"I-I-I'm sorry," Devon stuttered. "I'll have two large cinnamon lattes please, one with extra whipped cream."

Devon again looked curiously out the café's window but saw nothing, then went back to the table. "So you didn't see that? Just a few seconds ago?" Devon pointed to the window. "Someone was standing right there, just staring into the café, right at me!"

Elliot searched outside the window. "Are you talking about the trees and the cars outside?" He turned his eyes to Devon.

"Never mind. It was probably a cat or something." He could tell Elliot was getting bored with his antics. "Anyway, the lattes are almost done; you can pick them up at the front counter. I'm stepping out now, and I'll be back soon." He gave Elliot a handshake before hurrying out.

"Alright, bud, keep your phone on volume," Elliot called out before the café door shut.

Devon searched for the apartment's location through his cell phone GPS app. The GPS notified him that he had an estimated time of thirteen minutes before he'd arrive at the location. *Not too shabby.* The apartment was fairly close to the café. *I'm certain Samara will appreciate that.* He received a text message from her.

Hey, babe, I'll be at the café in five minutes.

Devon replied: *Okay, can't wait to see you.*

He sped up his pace, knowing Samara wasn't one to sit and wait patiently.

He rounded the corner on Bushwick Avenue. The street was shaded with tall oak trees; the houses were old, and some appeared abandoned. Devon continued to follow directions on his cell phone. He glanced up every once in a while, to admire the tall trees. *What an unusual neighborhood,* he thought to himself as leaves fluttered in the wind. He then remembered to share his location with Elliot. While doing so, Devon could hear the crunching dead leaves underneath his feet as he strolled. He lifted his head and realized someone was walking ahead. He stopped and looked around to see if he'd passed anyone, but there was no one else. *Is that the same person I saw outside the café window?*

His GPS suddenly recalculated his location. "Damn!"

He moved ahead to grab the attention of the stranger. "Hey, excuse me. Uh, sir or ma'am." The stranger suddenly stopped as Devon approached. Startled, Devon tripped over his own foot and fell to the ground. He quickly picked himself up in embarrassment, his face red. The stranger didn't move.

"Hello? Excuse me, can you help me out? I think I'm a little lost. My GPS gave out on me," Devon nervously chuckled as he waited for a reply.

The stranger slowly turned to face him. It was a man, but his dark black eyes were void. It was like staring into the eyes of death. Chills coursed down Devon's spine.

"I am sorry, sir. Never mind, sir. I think I've got it from here." He quickly walked away from the seemingly deranged stranger, glancing behind to see if the man would follow. The figure didn't budge.

That was freaky. Devon then received an alert on his cell, indicating he had arrived at his destination. He placed his phone in his pocket.

The house seemed completely normal from the outside. Devon found the front gate slightly open and gave it a hesitant push. He rang the doorbell and stood back for a moment. The door opened on its own, and there was no one to welcome him inside. Devon began to wonder if he should head back to the café and forget about the whole thing at this point. He reached for his phone and saw a new message appear in his inbox; it was Bella.

Dear Devon,
Please meet me inside once you've arrived. I'll be waiting for you in Apartment B3.

Devon slowly stepped inside and shut the door behind him. The inside of the building was in dire need of remodeling. The floors creaked with every step; the paint on the walls seemed to crumble. Devon discovered a dark stairwell leading to Apartment B3.

"Hello! Is anyone there?" he shouted, looking down the stairwell. He could see a dim light peeking through an open door. "Of course, the apartment would be all the way down there," he said out loud.

Taking a deep breath, he crept down the creaking staircase. Hesitating, Devon made his final step at the bottom of the stairs and walked inside the apartment, when suddenly, a strong, cold draft blew past him, slamming the door shut from behind. Alarmed, Devon turned back and tried to pull the door open, but it had locked itself from the outside. His heart began to pound in fear.

He heard a soft voice echoed: "Hello? Is that you?"

"Yes," his voice cracked, "it's me, Devon. I'm here. Bella?"

"You can come right in; don't be afraid," the woman's voice reassured.

Devon took a deep breath and started through the empty

apartment. He walked into what he believed to be the living room but didn't see anyone there.

"No. I am in the opposite direction," the voice giggled.

Devon reversed and went into the next room. *Why couldn't I just be greeted at the front entrance like a normal person?*

The apartment was surprisingly substantial, but there was no way he could imagine living here. *If I can just meet Bella and get this over with, I can focus on setting up a tour somewhere else—anywhere else but here!*

Devon reached for his phone but realized there was no reception inside the apartment. *Ugh, I am seriously screwed right now.* Following Bella's soft voice, he made his way to the kitchen, where he found her.

"Hello? Bella, right?" Devon asked.

Bella had her back to Devon. "Yes, it's me. So, what do you think?" she asked over her shoulder. The ceiling light made her long, silky hair gleam. She wore a short lace dress, revealing her striking figure.

Devon's gaze shifted as he exhaled a long breath. "Well, I'm so glad I found the place. There were so many trees on the avenue on my way here. I was afraid I'd miss it," Devon chuckled.

Still with her back to him, Bella spoke in a warm and gentle tone. "Here's a little treat for you. Just like I promised."

Bella slid a small mason jar to Devon across the kitchen's granite counter. He caught it before it hit the floor.

"Your reflexes are quite spot on, Devon. I'm impressed."

The jar was filled with berries, or at least that's what Devon thought they were. He brought the glass container up to his nose, giving a deep sniff, and reached inside to grab a berry.

"But aren't you going to ask me what they are?" Bella asked tentatively.

Devon took another look at the jar of berries in his hand. "Well, they're blueberries, of course." He paused while examining the jar. "Or they could very well be huckleberries?" Devon popped a couple more berries in his mouth and began to chew.

Bella finally turned around, giving Devon his first full glimpse of her. She was unlike anyone Devon had ever seen. He gaped at her, not believing his own eyes. She was a goddess. His eyes dazzled as Bella leaned over the counter and propped her chin on her hands.

"Do you like the taste?" Bella asked, raising one eyebrow.

Speechless, Devon ate the last berry.

"I'd love to show you around some more if you'd let me, Devon," she smirked.

Bella strolled elegantly to the next room as Devon followed behind. He took a deep breath, feeling betrayed by his heart as it began to race. Grabbing his chest, he thought maybe he'd been mesmerized by Bella's beauty.

"You know, Devon, I've shown plenty of young men like you this place," Bella said.

"And what happened with them?" Devon asked, trying not to sound overly interested.

"Well, they didn't necessarily fit my . . . preference." Bella paused and glared at Devon, watching as he followed her into the next room. "I didn't like them, so I had to get rid of them, right? And just like that, they were finished." She snapped her fingers. "But here you are," Bella gave Devon an evil grin, "and I think I like you," she giggled.

Bella's hips swayed as she strode over to Devon. She began to caress his back.

He swallowed hard, and his hands started to tremble.

"Ooh, Devon, you're so strong." Bella breathed in his scent and grasped his arm. "Do you like the way this feels?"

Devon looked around the room and nodded his head, speechless. *What the hell am I doing?* He began to sweat.

"Oh, are you feeling all right?" Bella gently held up Devon's chin for a better look. "You don't look so well."

Devon seemed to be dozing as his skin grew pale and his chest tight. "Stop." His voice was feeble as he turned his head to the doorway, wanting to leave the apartment.

"What was that? Are you trying to say something?" Bella gave him an icy stare. "I thought we were getting along just fine." She circled her arms around his neck and swayed side to side.

I can barely keep my eyes open. What is happening to me? He slipped away from Bella's arms and staggered to the door.

"WHERE DO YOU THINK YOU'RE GOING!" Bella bawled in a spine-chilling shriek; the sound of her voice sent shivers through Devon's body.

"I don't think I should be here," he said in a quavering voice, wiping sweat from his forehead. He tried to focus his blurred vision as he took off, running toward the door. He took one look behind and discovered that Bella had disappeared. There was a sudden stillness around him.

All the lights went out, and the apartment sank into cold

darkness. Devon froze with his hand on the doorknob. *Is this how I'm going to die?* He heard a voice whispering in tongues from behind. "Bella is that you?" he asked in a shaky breath, searching the darkness. Suddenly, a shadow appeared. Devon looked up at the shadow; the features were unclear.

"Bella? Look, if that's you, I'm no longer interested. I'd like to leave now, please." His voice was filled with fear.

The silent shadow manifested—it was Bella. With a dark stare, she was both riveting and frightening. Her skin crumpled and decayed from her body; her hair fell from her scalp. She groaned and let out a loud growl.

She was a succubus!

"Get out, get out, get out," she mocked in a deep, demonic voice, heading straight for Devon.

He huddled in a corner, terrified, squeezing his eyes shut. He remembered the night of his paralysis.

"It was you!" Devon screamed in terror as he opened his eyes. He struggled to pull the door open. His feet slid across the floor as he pushed and pulled with all his might. "Get me out of here!" He banged his fists on the door, but it would not open.

An ear-piercing scream echoed throughout the apartment, a scream so deafening that Devon dropped into a fetal position, trembling on the ground. He shut his eyes and covered his ears. "Let me out, you psycho!" he sobbed.

The screaming stopped, and Devon opened his eyes. He stood up and reached into his pocket for his cell phone, and his fingers found the onyx ring. He immediately felt a rush of adrenaline through his body as he held onto the ring. *This isn't an ordinary ring. Ms. James said I would need it for protection.*

Devon got up and pulled the door, swinging it open. His blurred vision was gone.

He looked to the dark stairwell and hurried up the creaking stairs. He struck his knee against one of the steps and stumbled, sending the ring soaring out of his hand and into the air. He felt his body grow weak, and again, his vision blurred. *Oh no, it's happening to me again. I need that ring!*

The succubus huddled in a dark corner at the bottom of the stairwell, feasting her eyes on Devon. She pulled back into a grotesque smile and then snapped her jaw shut.

Disoriented and weak, Devon's body slid down a few steps before he grounded near the bottom. He grunted and turned to his side; the onyx ring appeared beside him, faintly illuminating in the darkness. Devon tried to lift himself up but realized he couldn't move; a wicked laugh echoed through the dark stairwell.

Bella's disfigured form suddenly pulled itself out from the darkness and crawled onto Devon's body. Sliding her rotting fingers over Devon's lips, the succubus spoke: "Do I frighten you?" She revealed her razor teeth, dripping with thick, stringy saliva. "I love your soul," she whispered in Devon's ear.

I must get out of here! He managed to move his head slightly away from Bella's distorted face and saw the onyx ring still beside him. It had pulled nearer to him like a magnet. Bella quickly realized what Devon was trying to do. Her eyes rolled back as she slowly tilted her head to one side, the sound of her neck bone cracking. She sat her feet on Devon's chest and brought her face close to his.

"Don't you get it!" The succubus stared at Devon. "I need

blood. She salivated as her tongue slithered like a snake over her deteriorating lips. "Your blood! So sweet and young," she said, giggling. She leaned in closer and pressed her lips to Devon's ear, "Surprise. You're tonight's snack." Her demon eyes grew large as she smiled down at him.

Devon desperately tried to squirm his body away from the ravenous succubus. He looked again at the ring, wishing it was a little closer, when suddenly, it leaped into the air and right into Devon's hand. *I can't believe it.*

Bella let out a ferocious scream that shook the room. The door swung open and shut as the lights started to flicker. In the blink of an eye, Bella vanished—she was gone, just like that. Devon could finally move his body again.

"You will never have my blood!" Devon screamed. The lights switched back on, and he stared around the empty room. "Why don't you get on out of here and leave me alone!" He pounded his fist into his hand.

Catching his breath, he paused and looked at the ring as it shone brightly in his hand; he slid it on his finger.

"Thank you, Ms. James!" he said out loud. He ran up the stairwell and rushed out of the building, where Elliot and Samara surprised him at the entrance.

"Whoa! What the HELL are you doing here?" Devon asked, pushing Elliot back with both hands. Samara and Elliot burst into laughter.

"Okay, dude. First, you scared the living daylights out of us, and second, I have your location, remember? You were taking way too long; we had to come check on you." Elliot smiled and shrugged his shoulders.

Devon stepped out of the building, slamming the door shut behind him.

"You okay, baby?" Samara threw her arms around Devon and gave him a big squeeze. "Elliot told me what you were up to. I didn't know you wanted us to move in together."

Out of breath, Devon glared at Elliot. "Bro, so you told her?"

"I had to, man. She was interrogating me with all these questions. I don't do well with the questions—you know that. I had to tell her the truth. As you can see, it worked, too." Elliot pointed at Samara with her arms wrapped around Devon. "Are you all right, man? You ran out of there like you were running a marathon."

"Everything's fine . . . I just . . . I just wouldn't recommend this place to anybody," Devon said, looking into Samara's eyes. "Babe, I want you to know I did not write that—"

"Shh." Samara placed a finger over Devon's lips. "Let's just forget about that nonsense, okay? I believe you."

They began to walk away from the house, across the yard, and Devon shut the gate behind them. He turned around to take one last glance at the haunted building.

"Yo, bro. Let's go. I need to get out of here. Something about this neighborhood gives me the heebie-jeebies," Elliot whined.

"I'll be right there," Devon said, turning to catch up. They began walking toward Elliot's vehicle. The three got into the car; Samara cuddled with Devon in the back seat as Elliot hopped into the driver's seat.

Elliot was ready to drive off when his phone sent out an alarming notification. He looked down at his phone and turned to Devon and Samara. "After hearing about your plans to move in together, I think I am ready too."

"You can't live with us, E," Samara said.

"Of course not. I wouldn't want that." Elliot shook his head.

Devon gave Elliot his attention. "So, what are you planning to do?"

"Well, I actually began my search too, and I think I found a place. Hopefully not too far from you guys." His face was excited as he pulled out and began to drive.

"So, where exactly is this new place?" Devon asked.

"Bro, it's kind of funny you ask me that question because I actually do not know. Now I'm beginning to sound like you. But it came from a random agent."

Devon raised his eyebrows, realizing the story had started to sound familiar.

Elliot continued, "I honestly do not remember, you know, but whatever, right?"

Devon interrupted Elliot and leaned forward. "E, what was the name they gave you. The name of the agent?"

"Uh, you know, I don't know that either," Elliot laughed out loud. "I know it's a woman. Hold on, I think I have her name. We've been chatting via email since last night. Let me check my inbox. He opened the message and began to read out loud.

Dear Elliot,
I look forward to tomorrow. We can meet in the evening, say 5:30 p.m.? I'll provide the location in another email. Please also remember, no unexpected visitors are allowed during tours! Can't wait.
PS Tours come with a special tasty treat.

Yours faithfully,
Belladonna

TO BE CONTINUED…

www.ingramcontent.com/pod-product-compliance
Lightning Source LLC
LaVergne TN
LVHW042003060526
838200LV00041B/1846